FUNNY JOKES

FOR

11

YEAR OLD KIDS

HUNDREDS OF HiLARiOUS JOKES iNSiDE!

JIMMY JONES

Hundreds of really funny, hilarious jokes that will have the kids in fits of laughter in no time!

They're all in here - the funniest
- Jokes
- Riddles
- Tongue Twisters
- Knock Knock Jokes

for 11 year old kids!

Funny kids love funny jokes and this brand new collection of original and classic jokes promises hours of fun for the whole family!

Books by Jimmy Jones

Funny Jokes For Funny Kids
Knock Knock Jokes For Funny Kids

Funny Jokes For Kids Series
All Ages 5 -12!

To see all the latest books by
Jimmy Jones just go to
kidsjokebooks.com

Contents

Funny Jokes!

Why did the spaceship want to play football?

So it could do a touchdown!

Why was the chicken on the soccer field?

The referee called fowl!

What did the girl font say to the boy font?

You are just my type!

Why did the fireman ring in sick?
He was feeling burned out!

Which dinosaur wore reading glasses?
A Tyrannosaurus Specs!

Why are dalmatians no good at hiding?
They are easy to spot!

If everybody had a white car what would we have?

A white carnation!

What do you call a camel crossed with a fish?

A humpback whale!

What do you get if you cross a boomerang with a Christmas present?

A gift that returns itself!

Why was the car muffler so tired?

He was exhausted!

What do you call a girl with one foot on one side of a stream and one foot on the other side?

Bridget!

What happened to the 2 rabbits when they fell in love?

They lived hoppily ever after!

What do you call a girl with one really short leg?

Eileen! (I lean)

What do you call a ship that has sunk and shivers on the bottom of the sea?

A nervous wreck!

Why did the bacteria travel across the microscope?

So he could get to the other slide!

How can you tell when a train is eating its lunch?

It goes choo-choo!

Why did the teacher go to the pool?

To test the water!

What did the doctor say to the patient who had a weird ringing in his ear?

Have you tried answering it?

What do you call a lady on a tennis court?
Annette! (A net!)

Why did the 2 science teachers get along so well?
They had great chemistry!

What do you call a thief?
Rob!

What do you call an elephant that didn't have a bath for a year?

A smellyphant!

What was the drummer's favorite vegetable?

Beets!

How did the plumber get to school?

On the tool bus!

Why did the boy go to the music store to get a cat?

He wanted a trum-pet!

Why did the clock have a holiday?

He needed to unwind!

Why did the beaver become an astronaut?

So he could go to otter space!

Which state has really small cans of soft drink?

Mini Soda!

Why did Darth Vader feel strange when Luke got him a gift for Christmas?

He felt his presents!

What did the skeleton chef say to his customers?

Bone appetit!

Where did the baby monster go when his mom was at work?

The Day Scare Centre!

What can you use to open the great lakes?

The Florida Keys!

Why was the Egyptian boy so sad?

His dad was a mummy!

What did the magical tractor do last Saturday?

Turned into a corn field!

What do you call a cactus crossed with a pig?

A porkerpine!

Why don't elephants get paid much?

They work for peanuts!

What did the panda say on Halloween night?

Bam-BOOO!

Why did Cinderella leave the basketball team?

She always ran away from the ball!

How did the cheese feel after a massage?

Grate!

Why was the computer tired when she got home from work?

She had a hard drive!

Which dessert is no fun to eat?

Apple Grumble!

What has one horn and lots of milk?

A milk truck!

Why didn't the moon finish its dinner?

It was full!

What did the cat say when the boy stepped on its tail?

Me-ow!

Which piece of a computer is an alien's favorite?

The space bar!

Why didn't the Egyptian mummies ever take time off?

They were scared to unwind!

How can you learn how to make a banana split?

Go to sundae school!

Why did the banana end up in hospital?

It wasn't peeling very well!

Why was the otter such a hard worker?

He was an eager beaver!

When is it bad luck if a black cat follows you?

When you are a grey mouse!

What kind of underwear did the reporter wear on TV?

News briefs!

Why doesn't Peter Pan ever stop flying?
He Neverlands!

Why did the girl love her cat?
She was purr-fect!

What did the carrot and the tomato say to the celery?
Quit stalking us!

What do you call a nose with no body, no head or eyes - just a nose?

Nobody nose!

Why did the pirate stop playing cards?

He was standing on the deck!

What is small, round, white, lives in a jar and giggles?

A tickled onion!

What did the pencil say to the pen?
Write on brother!

What do cats eat for desert?
Mice cream!

Why was the computer sneezing all day?
It had a really bad virus!

What do you call a football playing cat?

Puss in boots!

Why did the rooster stop crossing the road?

He was too chicken!

What would happen if you crossed a centipede with a parrot?

You get a walkie talkie!

Who eats at the restaurant on the bottom of the sea?

Scuba diners!

Where did the alien get a coffee?

Starbucks!

How did the math teacher know the girl was lying?

Her story didn't add up!

How do you stop a skunk from smelling?
Hold its nose!

What lies in a pram and wobbles?
A Jelly Baby!

Why did the orange fall asleep at school?
She ran out of juice!

Why did the vampire get in big trouble at the blood bank?

He was drinking on the job!

What do you call a dinosaur who is going to have a baby next week?

A Preggosaurus!

Where did the bird invest his savings?

In the stork market!

What roads do ghosts like to haunt?
Dead ends!

Why are ghosts no good at lying?
You can usually see right through them!

What did the big wall say to the smaller wall?
Let's catch up at the corner!

What is a nut with facial hair called?
A mustachio!

Why did the couple stop doing laundry?
They just threw in the towel!

Why did Cinderella leave the basketball team?
She always ran away from the ball!

Why did the lion try to eat a Ferrari?
He was a Car-nivore!

What did the doctor say to the patient who thought he was an elevator?
Lucky you can stop at this floor!

What do you call an auto mechanic?
Axel!

What do you get if you cross a duck with a rooster?

A bird that wakes you up at the

quack of dawn!

What do you call a really nutty girl?

Hazel!

What is a cat's favorite car?

CAT-illacs!

What did the vampire get when he bit the snowman?

Frostbite!

What do crabs do on their birthday?

They shell-abrate!

What do you call a snowman with dandruff?

Snowflakes!

Funny Knock Knock Jokes!

Knock knock.

Who's there?

Poll.

Poll who?

Poll iceman John here!

You're under arrest!

Knock knock.

Who's there?

Havana.

Havana who?

I'm Havana great time out here!

Knock knock.

Who's there?

Yeast.

Yeast who?

The yeast you can do is let me in!

I've been waiting for ages!

Knock knock.

Who's there?

Lefty.

Lefty who?

Lefty key at home so I had to knock!

Knock knock.

Who's there?

Baby owl.

Baby owl who?

Baby owl see you at school next week!

Knock knock.

Who's there?

Gopher.

Gopher who?

Gopher help quick!

My foot is stuck!

Knock knock.

Who's there?

Mandy.

Mandy who?

Mandy lifeboats! We're sinking!

Knock knock.

Who's there?

Cheese.

Cheese who?

For cheese a jolly good fellow, for cheese a jolly good fellow!!

Knock knock.

Who's there?

Attilla.

Attilla who?

Attilla you no lies if you aska me no questions!

Knock knock.

Who's there?

Mikey.

Mikey who?

Mikey doesn't fit!

Why did you change the lock?

Knock knock.

Who's there?

Pudding.

Pudding who?

Pudding my new shoes on.

Do you like them?

Knock knock.

Who's there?

Egg.

Egg who?

It's so Eggciting to see you again!

Knock knock.

Who's there?

Hank.

Hank who?

You are so welcome sir!

Knock knock.

Who's there?

Ivan.

Ivan who?

Ivan appointment to see you today!

Are you free now?

Knock knock.

Who's there?

Eggs.

Eggs who?

Its eggs-tremely hot out here so please let me in!

Knock knock.

Who's there?

Bat.

Bat who?

Bat you will never guess who it is!

It's me!

Knock knock.

Who's there?

Jamaican.

Jamaican who?

Jamaican dinner?

Yummy!

Knock knock.

Who's there?

Ahmed.

Ahmed who?

Ahmed a mistake! Sorry!

Wrong house!

Knock knock.

Who's there?

Heaven.

Heaven who?

Heaven seen you in ages!

You're looking good!

Knock knock.

Who's there?

Leaf.

Leaf who?

If we Leaf now we can get there on

time!

Knock knock.

Who's there?

Ice cream.

Ice cream who?

Ice cream when I jump in the pool!

It's fun!

Knock knock.

Who's there?

Canoe.

Canoe who?

Canoe help me fix my flat tire?

Knock knock.

Who's there?

Candice.

Candice who?

Candice door open any faster if I push it?

Knock knock.

Who's there?

Sawyer.

Sawyer who?

Sawyer lights on so I thought I would knock!

Knock knock.

Who's there?

Witches.

Witches who?

Witches the fastest way to my house from here?

Knock knock.

Who's there?

Abel.

Abel who?

Abel would mean I don't have to knock!

Knock knock.

Who's there?

Heaven.

Heaven who?

I'm Heaven a party on Friday.

Want to come?

Knock knock.

Who's there?

Sadie.

Sadie who?

Sadie magic word and your wish will

come true!

Knock knock.

Who's there?

Ben.

Ben who?

Ben knocking so long I forgot why

I'm here!

Knock knock.

Who's there?

Design.

Design who?

Design says you are open for lunch!

I'm really hungry!

Knock knock.

Who's there?

Annie.

Annie who?

Annie idea when this rain will stop?

I'm getting wet!

Knock knock.

Who's there?

Hawaii.

Hawaii who?

Great thanks, Hawaii you?

Knock knock.

Who's there?

Tank.

Tank who?

Tank goodness you finally answered the door!

Knock knock.

Who's there?

Scold.

Scold who?

Scold enough today to make a snowman!

Knock knock.

Who's there?

Gorilla.

Gorilla who?

I can gorilla burger for your lunch if you like! Yummy!

Knock knock.

Who's there?

House.

House who?

House it going my oldest friend?

Knock knock.

Who's there?

Eiffel.

Eiffel who?

Eiffel down and hurt my knee!

Owwwww!

Knock knock.

Who's there?

Eliza.

Eliza who?

Eliza quite a bit so I never believe him!

Knock knock.

Who's there?

Zesty.

Zesty who?

Zesty right place for the birthday party?

Knock knock.

Who's there?

Teresa.

Teresa who?

Teresa very green this time of year!

Knock knock.

Who's there?

Kermit.

Kermit who?

Kermit any crimes and the police will get you!

Knock knock.

Who's there?

Kent.

Kent who?

Kent you see I want to come in!

I've been waiting for 3 hours!

Knock knock.

Who's there?

Jim.

Jim who?

Jim mind if I stay for a while?

I got locked out of my own house!

Knock knock.

Who's there?

Stopwatch.

Stopwatch who?

Stopwatch you're doing!

The bus is here!

Knock knock.

Who's there?

Adam.

Adam who?

If you Adam up I'll pay half the bill!

Knock knock.

Who's there?

Duncan.

Duncan who?

Duncan a cookie in milk is fun!

Knock knock.

Who's there?

Imma.

Imma who?

Imma getting a bit wet out here in the rain! Please let me in!

Knock knock.

Who's there?

Pecan.

Pecan who?

Pecan someone your own size you bully!

Knock knock.

Who's there?

Amin.

Amin who?

Amin already so don't worry about

the door!

Knock knock.

Who's there?

Abby.

Abby who?

Abby stung me on my foot.

OWWWWWWWWWW!!

Knock knock.

Who's there?

Diet.

Diet who?

You can change your hair color if you diet!

Knock knock.

Who's there?

Viper.

Viper who?

Viper nose before you get sick!

Knock knock.

Who's there?

Amos.

Amos who?

Amos say you look great in that suit!

Where did you get it?

Knock knock.

Who's there?

CD.

CD who?

CD car out the front?

That's my new car! Woo Hoo!

Knock knock.

Who's there?

Bean.

Bean who?

Bean waiting here for ages!

Why are you always so late?

Knock knock.

Who's there?

Matthew.

Matthew who?

Matthew lace has come undone!

Noooo!

Knock knock.

Who's there?

Izzy.

Izzy who?

Izzy doorbell working yet?

It's been 3 years!

Knock knock.

Who's there?

Who Who.

Who Who Who?

How long have you had a pet owl?

Knock knock.

Who's there?

Alex.

Alex who?

Alex plain it all to you in a minute!

Please let me in!

Knock knock.

Who's there?

Jimmy.

Jimmy who?

Jimmy 2 seconds and I will tell you

all about it!

Funny Riddles!

What do you call it when 10 people go to a disco?

Attendance.

What do you call a bike that can bite you?

A vicious cycle!

When does B come after U?

When you take its honey!

The more you take, the more you leave behind. What am I?

Footsteps!

What has 1 head, 4 legs and 1 foot?

A bed!

If a man is born in Canada, grows up in Australia and dies in America, what is he?

Dead!

Where do most kings and queens get crowned?

On their heads!

What do you call a stick of dynamite that comes back when you throw it away?

A BOOMerang!

What tastes better than it smells?

Your tongue!

How many antelope are there in the world?
About a gazelle-ion!

What is the smartest insect?
The brilli-ant!

How did the girl invite the fish to her birthday?
She dropped it a line!

How can you spell cold with only 2 letters?
I C (icy)!

What is the best day for a rabbit to have a haircut?

When they are having a bad hare

day!

How to people on saturn communicate?
They give each other a ring!

What has many rings but no fingers?
A telephone!

What do girls always leave behind at the beach?
Footprints!

Why did the horse orbit the earth?
To be a saddle-ite!

How do we know carrots are good for our eyes?

Because rabbits never wear glasses!

What begins with T, ends with T and has T in it?

Teapot!

What can you serve but never eat?

A tennis ball!

What do you call 2 pigs that share a room?
Pen pals!

What starts with "e" and ends with "e" but contains only one letter?
An envelope!

What goes up when water comes down?
An umbrella!

What gets bigger the more you take away from it?

A hole!

What is as big as a bus but weighs nothing?

Its shadow!

Which fruit is never alone, even if there is only one?

A pear!

When is a door not a door?
When it is ajar!

What can you break without even touching it?
A promise!

What has 2 legs but can't walk?
A pair of jeans!

Where do aliens live?
Green houses!

What can you hold without touching it?
Your breath!

What went into the lion's cage, stayed for 3 hours and came out with no scratches?
A bigger lion!

What did the slug do before her first date?
Put on some snail varnish!

What does everyone have but never lose?
Their shadow!

How many sheep does it take to make 3 woolly jumpers?
None. Sheep can't knit!

Funny Tongue Twisters!

Tongue Twisters are great fun!
Start off slow.
How fast can you go?

Five free frogs.
Five free frogs.
Five free frogs.

Bubble blubber.
Bubble blubber.
Bubble blubber.

Swiss wrist watches.
Swiss wrist watches.
Swiss wrist watches.

Gum glue grew.
Gum glue grew.
Gum glue grew.

Lick yellow lollies.
Lick yellow lollies.
Lick yellow lollies.

Three fleas fly.
Three fleas fly.
Three fleas fly.

Bad money, mad bunny.
Bad money, mad bunny.
Bad money, mad bunny.

Sammy likes slimy slugs.
Sammy likes slimy slugs.
Sammy likes slimy slugs.

Bring the black boot back.
Bring the black boot back.
Bring the black boot back.

Stupid superstitions.
Stupid superstitions.
Stupid superstitions.

Fry fish freshly.
Fry fish freshly.
Fry fish freshly.

Shoe section.
Shoe section.
Shoe section.

Watching washing wash.
Watching washing wash.
Watching washing wash.

Swan swam over the sea.
Swan swam over the sea.
Swan swam over the sea.

Five fleeing frantic frogs.
Five fleeing frantic frogs.
Five fleeing frantic frogs.

My short suit shrunk.
My short suit shrunk.
My short suit shrunk.

She sees cheese.
She sees cheese.
She sees cheese.

Blow blue bubbles.
Blow blue bubbles.
Blow blue bubbles.

Sly sheep should sleep.
Sly sheep should sleep.
Sly sheep should sleep.

She sees seas slapping shores.
She sees seas slapping shores.
She sees seas slapping shores.

A proper copper coffee pot.
A proper copper coffee pot.
A proper copper coffee pot.

Frog flip frog.
Frog flip frog.
Frog flip frog.

The gum glue grew glum.
The gum glue grew glum.
The gum glue grew glum.

Bonus Funny Jokes!

How does a bee get to work?
She waits at the buzz stop!

Why did the man marry the barbecue?
She was the grill of his dreams!

What did the frustrated magician do?
Pulled out his hare!

How did the frog die?
He just croaked it!

What is a chicken's favorite type of car?
A coop!

Why did the man get rid of his beard?
He had a close shave!

What happened to the ghost comedian?
He was booed off stage!

Why did the bird book into the hospital?
To get some tweetment!

What scary creature lives in your keyboard?
The Caps Loch Ness Monster!

What did the doctor say to the patient who forgot where he put his boomerang?

I'm sure it will come back to you!

What do you get if you cross a dinosaur with a policeman?

A Tricera-cops!

Why did the chicken go for a jog?

She needed the egg-cersize!

Which animal appears on legal documents?
A seal!

What do ghosts eat for lunch?
Spook-getthi!

What do you call an adult bear that has no teeth?
The gummy bear!

How did the angel light her camp fire?
She used a match made in heaven!

Why was it so hot at the basketball game?
Most of the fans had left!

Why was the snowman lonely?
He was ice-olated!

What did the doctor say to the patient who thought he was a dog?

Sit!

What happens if there is a fight in the fish and chip shop?

The fish get battered!

Why was the atom sure it lost an electron?

It was positive!

What do you call a pig that can do kung fu?
A pork chop!

What do you call a frog sitting on a chair?
A toadstool!

Why was the boy so wet when he got to school?
He came in a car pool!

What do you call a skeleton that sleeps in?
Lazy Bones!

What did the bee say when he got home from work?
Honey, I'm home!

Why did the duck cross the road?
The chicken had the day off!

What do toads play after school?
Leapfrog!

What did the music teacher put on her bed?
Sheet music!

What did the can of soda study at college?
Fizzics!

Where is Dracula's office?

The Vampire State Building!

What do you call a man who lives in the toilet?

John!

What is the best place for an elephant to store her luggage?

In her trunk!

Why did the pony stop singing in the farm band?

She was a little hoarse!

What sort of music do frogs listen to?

Hip Hop!

Why are poodles so good to be around?

They are very paws-itive!

Bonus

Knock Knock Jokes!

Knock knock.

Who's there?

Abby.

Abby who?

Abby new year! Let's celebrate!

Knock knock.

Who's there?

Barbie.

Barbie who?

Barbie Q for dinner! Yummy!

Knock knock.

Who's there?

Fork.

Fork who?

Fork got to mention, why is your doorbell broken?

Knock knock.

Who's there?

Wanda.

Wanda who?

I Wanda what we can do with all this money my aunt gave me?

Knock knock.

Who's there?

Urine.

Urine who?

Urine a lot of trouble if you don't

open this door!

Knock knock.

Who's there?

Wooden.

Wooden who?

Wooden you like to let me in so I can

give you your present?

Knock knock.

Who's there?

Chicken.

Chicken who?

I'm chicken under the mat and I can't

find the key! Noooo!

Knock knock.

Who's there?

Argo.

Argo who?

Argo to school in the morning,

but first I need some sleep!

Knock knock.

Who's there?

Buster.

Buster who?

I'm catching the Buster school tomorrow. How about you?

Knock knock.

Who's there?

Butcher.

Butcher who?

Butcher right leg in, Butcher right leg out...!

Knock knock.

Who's there?

Tweet.

Tweet who?

Would you like tweet an apple?

They are really tasty!

Knock knock.

Who's there?

Dishes.

Dishes who?

Dishes me, remember?

We met last week!

Knock knock.

Who's there?

Earl.

Earl who?

Earl be very happy when you let me in!

Knock knock.

Who's there?

Ariel.

Ariel who?

Ariel lly want to come inside so let me in!

Knock knock.

Who's there?

Ken.

Ken who?

Ken I please have a drink?

I am so thirsty!

Knock knock.

Who's there?

Eddy.

Eddy who?

Eddy body home?

I ran out of food!

Knock knock.

Who's there?

Candy.

Candy who?

Candy door be answered faster next time please?

Knock knock.

Who's there?

Tunis.

Tunis who?

Tunis company but three's a crowd!

Knock knock.

Who's there?

Athena.

Athena who?

Athena shooting star last night so I made a wish!

Knock knock.

Who's there?

Will.

Will who?

Will you marry me?

I love you so much!

Knock knock.

Who's there?

Leon.

Leon who?

You can Leon me if your leg is still sore!

Knock knock.

Who's there?

Lettuce.

Lettuce who?

Please lettuce in before our ice cream melts!

Knock knock.

Who's there?

Ida.

Ida who?

Ida like to speak with you about our new range of doorbells!

Knock knock.

Who's there?

Emerson.

Emerson who?

Emerson nice socks you have on. Did you get them at Kmart?

Thank you so much

For reading our book.

I hope you have enjoyed these funny jokes for 11 year old kids as much as my kids and I did as we were putting this book together.

We really had a lot of fun and laughter creating and compiling this book and we really appreciate you for reading our book.

If you could possibly let us know what you thought of our book by way of a review we would really appreciate it 😊

To see all our latest books or leave a review just go to
kidsjokebooks.com
Once again, thanks so much for reading.

All the best,
Jimmy Jones
And also Ella & Alex (the kids)
And even Obi (the dog – he's very cute!)

Printed in Great Britain
by Amazon